THE
FAITHFUL HUNTER
Abenaki Stories

THE
FAITHFUL HUNTER
Abenaki Stories

As Told By
JOSEPH BRUCHAC
Illustrations by Kahionhes

Greenfield Review Press
Greenfield Center, New York

Bowman Books #3
ISBN 0-912678-75-5

"The Faithful Hunter" and "How Indian Summer Came to Be" first appeared in *Rooted Like the Ash Trees*. Eagle Wing Press 1987.

Design by Patrick J. Powers
Set by Sans Serif Typesetters, Ann Arbor, Michigan

Bowman Books is an imprint of The Greenfield Review Press. All of the volumes in the series are devoted to contemporary retelling of traditional tales.

The Greenfield Review Press
P.O. Box 308
2 Middle Grove Road
Greenfield Center, NY 12833

Distribution by
The Talman Co., Inc.
131 Spring Street
New York, NY 10012
(212) 431-7175   FAX (212) 431-7215

*This book is dedicated to
the children of Missisquoi and Odanak
and to those who have remained
faithful to the people of the land.*

LEGEND

WABANAKI COUNTRY

MICMAC TRIBAL NAMES

——--- NATIONAL BOUNDARY (U.S / CANADA)

——--- STATE AND PROVINCIAL BOUNDARIES

● PRESENT DAY CITIES

MONTAGNAIS / NASKAPI

ST. L

CANADA
U.S.A.

QUEBEC ●

ALGONKIN

CHAUDIERE R.

PA
AROOSTO
U.S.

NORRIDGEWOCK

PENOBSCOT

PENOBSCOT

AROSAGUNTICOOK
(ST. FRANCIS)

MONTREAL ●

RICHELIEU R.

ST. FRANCIS R.

MISSISQUOI R.

LAKE
CHAMPLAIN

KENNEBEC R.

MISSISQOIK

COWASUCK

PIGWACKET

CONNECTICUT RIVER

ANDROSCOGGIN R.

WAWENOCK

CANADA
U.S.A.

GANIENKEHAGA
(MOHAWK)

SOKWAKI

PEN A COOK

MERRIMACK R.

MAHICAN

HUDSON RIVER

WAPPINGER

N I P M U C

BOSTON ●
PLYMOUTH ●

WAMPANOAG

CAPE COD

MOHEGAN /
PEQUOT

NARRAGANSETT

NEW YORK

A

W

A

B

A

JUNE, 1988

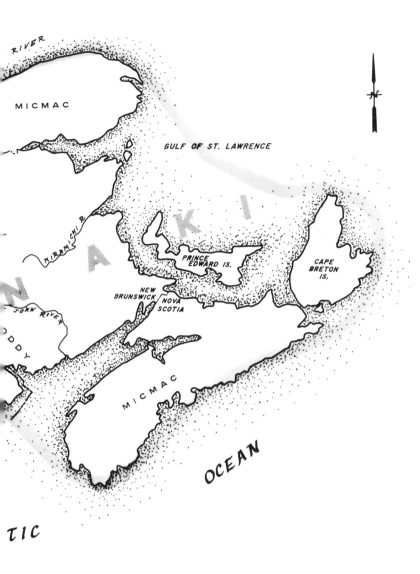

RIVER

MICMAC

GULF OF ST. LAWRENCE

N

MIRAMICHI R.

A

K

I

PRINCE
EDWARD IS.

CAPE
BRETON
IS.

NEW
BRUNSWICK

NOVA
SCOTIA

JOHN RIVER

ODDY

MICMAC

OCEAN

TIC

WABANAKI COUNTRY
THE WABANAKI
AND THEIR NATIVE AMERICAN NEIGHBORS
⇉ FROM ANCIENT TIMES TO THE EARLY 18th CENTURY ⇇

CARTOGRAPHY BY: STACY MORIN, COUNTRY
RDS. INC., ORRINGTON, ME.

SCALE

0   20   40   60   80   100 MI.

INTRODUCTION

Four years ago, Joe Bruchac and John Kahionhes Fadden produced a remarkable work of 'Gluskabe stories' called the *Wind Eagle* which told and illustrated how life in Wabanaki, the Dawn Land, began many thousands of years ago. With *The Faithful Hunter*, the two have once more collaborated to show and retell the Abenaki stories of life in the ancient times.

Relationships, relations, are the center of this work. Old, sacred, and funny relations between the plants, trees and animals, weave for the reader a tapestry of Wabanaki values and insight. The quiet, open handed retelling of these stories is an invitation to find a way to live without destroying the ancient roots of ways that have sustained human beings here for thousands of years. Being a work largely written in one of the western European languages, the book itself continues the crucial task of fostering understanding and peaceful relations between Native Americans and we newcomers from Africa, Asia and Europe. The stories also serve to remind us of how important all of our most ancient traditions are. From stories of the plants, animals, family, and the land, grow the potential for our collective survival, and freedom, for another hundred, or thousand years.

Like the *Wind Eagle*, this second set of Wabanaki stories reveal how the world from Bitawbagok (Lake Champlain) east to Sobagw (Atlantic Ocean) was transformed into a place, and way of being, where the Wabanaki people could live. The coming of night and day, and the early origins of the sacred sweet grass, are woven into the story of Gluscabe and the Skunk. Sweet grass is one of the ancient aromatics. Like cedar, and sage, it is still used in daily, and ceremonial life and art among many of the northeastern Native American peoples. In another story of how the Wabanakiak, the People from the Dawnland, were created out of the ash tree, comes an understanding of the fundamental Abenaki cultural identity.

The Faithful Hunter story, from which this work takes its title, clearly underscores the family responsibilities of the Abenaki husband and father. The stories of Gluskabe and the baby, Dzidziz, as well as those of Gluskabe and the Maple Trees, Gluskabe and the Four Wishes, The Deer Wife, How Indian Summer Came To Be and Pmola and the Hunter, amplify this theme of the family's central importance in Abenaki life. And they exemplify the most honored tradition of quiet forbearance and deep loyalty to family and friend common to all the Wabanaki peoples.

In the four interconnected stories of Azeban we are also introduced to the humorous antics of the eastern Trickster, Raccoon. One version of this sequence of stories was centered at Dagwahoganek, often called Taquahunga, or Swanton Falls, at Missisquoi in northwestern Vermont. If the Wabanaki are a quiet, reserved people, sometimes depicted as fierce defenders of their ancestral lands and families, the Azeban tales confirm their love and appreciation of openhearted, good humor as well. And these stories also reveal some of the underlying beliefs in humility and balance common to Wabanaki lifeways.

This work also confirms a basic truth of northeastern history: peacemaking and close cultural and familial ties between the ancient, original peoples of this land. It is clear that the Missisquoi, Lake George/Saratoga and other western Abenakis, with their Mahican cousins, and the Ganienkehaga, eastern doorkeepers of the Hodenausaunee, had an extensive and peaceful history of shared life centered around the northern New York and northern New England/southern Quebec region. The key to these relations, despite periods of tension, were families which bridged the international boundary between the Iroquoian and Algonquin peoples along the Champlain and Hudson River valleys. To this day, many of the Ganienhehaga of New York and Quebec know their Abenaki, particularly, western Abenaki ancestry, and many Abenakis derive in part from Ganienhehaga ancestors. These families maintained contact in war and peace, bridging the challenging gaps fostered by international warfare in the 17th, 18th and 19th centuries.

A map of Wabanaki country is also enclosed here. It should be understood that there were many more villages and peoples found in the region anciently. This map just shows the major surviving groups now known to non-Indian governments and historians. Every region of the northeast has families and enclaves of the Wabanaki within, as well as outside, their traditional, national territories, where they lived, and in many cases, continue to live today. In addition, the Wabanaki are found in virtually every city and non-Indian town in the northeast. And, being great travelers since ancient times, their families and descendants can now be found in many areas of the globe within, and outside the Americas.

There is an urgency reflected here in these ancient stories about the seasons of change. To many Wabanakis, the past few hundred years have been like a winter of the soul which must be turned to spring with extraordinary effort. Behind the lengthy legacy of Native American dispossession, holocaust and disaspora, come these stories of survival and regeneration. These stories carry one paramount message to the European newcomers, in particular, that there is a crying need for balance in our relations with all aspects of creation. A similar theme is found in Asian, African and ancient European traditions from the times when human life around the world was tied to the seasonal round. In The Deer Wife, relations between humans and our close mammalian relatives are carefully compared to those between woman and man. Always, the story councils, there must be a balance between the demands of our own, human life and society, with those of the earth we live on and depend upon for our food, shelter and the good life.

A great deal remains to be done. It has just now become customary in portions of the northeast, for Wabanaki and other burial grounds and sacred sites to be protected from destruction or desecration. Still, many of the ancient subsistence, healing and spiritual practices of the Wabanaki are suppressed or considered to be illegal in all or part of non-Indian society.

In New England, and Canada both, some legal and political victories by the tribes have made them major factors in the economic and cultural life of the region, but most of the families and communities retain the sense of layered injustices and oppression needing to be healed. Ironically, generations of open, caring non-Indians in the northeast have long since inspired a renaissance of Native American ecological, political and spiritual values which has touched all walks of life. From the old hunting, fishing, trapping, gathering and gardening ways shared with the early non-Indian settlers, to the tremendous growth of whole system ecological awareness and conservationism, the northeast has become a place of hope reflected in a mass re-migration back into the wilderness and rural areas.

However, that deep hunger for a quiet, Indian-style life, has come at a stiff price. It has generated unprecedented development pressures on the Adirondacks and northern New England region, as well as portions of Wabanaki country in Canada. Just as the moose, wolf, coyote, bear, deer, eagle, peregrine and countless other creatures are finding the reforested and open lands of the northeast home again, migration from urban areas is gobbling up these farmlands and forests in an almost frenetic, driven fashion.

No where in the world has there ever been a clear, popular return to the ancient, individual and family values of forbearance and balance with the ecology which is now needed to protect and preserve this world for future generations. Where governments can reflect the will of humans, and perhaps, help in the protection of the land, waters and air, it is the collective awareness and will of humans which holds the most hope, and creative potential, for our future. These stories are clear, and ancient reminders of the need for balance, forethought, clarity, humility and humor in our relations with *all* creation, including the earth we all live on. Listen well.

John Moody
Sharon, Vermont
October 18, 1988

CONTENTS

THE STORIES

Gluskabe and Skunk	5
Gluskabe Makes the People	9
Gluskabe Changes the Animals	11
Gluskabe and the Maple Trees	15
Gluskabe and Dzidziz	19
Gluskabe's Uncle Turtle and the Birds	23
Gluskabe and the Four Wishes	27
Azaban the Raccoon	33
Pmola and the Hunter	49
The Faithful Hunter	53
The Deer Wife	55
How Indian Summer Came To Be	59

TELLING STORIES

Wherever I've visited Native American people, I've heard stories. Sometimes they've been told in traditional settings—in a sweat lodge or around a fire. Other times I've listened to stories in a house trailer sitting at a kitchen table while people in the next room watched TV. (Though when the storytelling began, the TV room was soon deserted.) The strength of traditional tales has not diminished, though the settings of Native American life may change. The stories last because of their continuing role in American Indian life. They entertain, they instruct, and they empower. Although told first for Native American people, they also may be of use to any human being who wishes to live in a good relationship with the world and the beings around us.

Among the people of the Northeast, the Iroquois and the Abenaki, the storyteller was often an older relative, perhaps a grandparent, an aunt or uncle, someone who remembered the stories from long ago. Although young people learned stories at an early age, it was almost always one of the older men or women who did the actual telling, since elders were always treated with great deference. Often that person would be careful to begin by saying "I cannot tell these tales as they used to be told," since boasting was frowned upon, even by a gifted storyteller.

There were also those who were more or less "professional" storytellers. Since they travelled about from place to place, these storytellers were usually men of vigorous health in late middle age. Among the Seneca nation of the Iroquois, such as storyteller was known as "Hageota." Among the Penobscot nation of the Wabanaki, a storyteller was called "Nudatlogit." Both mean a person who carries stories. Those storytellers often would carry a storytelling pouch, filled with such things

1

as animal claws, various feathers, a corn husk doll, a flint arrowhead—items which would remind the storyteller of a particular legend when he pulled something out at random. Good luck was said to follow a good storyteller and he was welcomed wherever he travelled. After the stories, those who had gathered to take part in the experience would each give the storyteller a small present, perhaps a bundle of tobacco or some beads.

In the old days, storytellers interacted with the people. Every now and then the storyteller might ask a question—expecting an answer from his participant audience—or say a word such as this: "Ho?" And those who were still awake and listening would answer "Henh!"

Ho?

THE STORIES

GLUSKABE AND SKUNK

Wowigit notlokgan wa Gluskabe. Here camps my story of Gluskabe. In the old days, Skunk was one of the most beautiful animals. His coat was made of pure white fur which was long and silky. All the animals admired him.

One day, Skunk went to visit Gluskabe. "Let me stay with you," Skunk said. "I would like to travel around with you. If you let me stay I will cook all of your meals for you."

Gluskabe was a little bit lazy. The thought of not having to cook pleased him. "Yes," Gluskabe said. "You may stay with me for a while."

For a time things went well. Skunk cooked fine meals which Gluskabe sat around and smoked his stone pipe. Before long, though, Gluskabe had to travel around again.

"There is too much snow falling," Gluskabe said. "I must go and speak to the Snow Bird.

"Let me travel with you," Skunk said.

Gluskabe tried to refuse. He told Skunk the trip would be long and cold. Skunk was stubborn, though, and finally Gluskabe agreed. The two of them began to walk along together. As they went along the snow got deeper. Now it was above Gluskabe's knees, but he still kept walking. Now it was above his waist, but he kept on walking still. It was very hard for Skunk, who had to struggle along in Gluskabe's big footprints. He began to get angry at Gluskabe. He forgot that it was his own idea to come along.

At last they came to the hilltop where a great white bird stood. As it spread its wings snow flakes fell from them.

"Kuai! Grandfather," Gluskabe said.

"Ah, Gluskabe," said the Snow Bird. "Why have you come."

"There is too much snow, Grandfather," said Gluskabe. "If it snows like this it will be hard for my children and my children's children to live." He bent over and pulled Skunk, who was almost frozen, out of the deep snow. "See how hard it is for my little brother here?"

The Snow Bird nodded. "I see," he said. Then he folded his wings and the snow stopped. To this day snow only falls part of the year because Gluskabe and Skunk visited the Snow Bird.

As they walked back to Gluskabe's lodge, the Skunk was thinking. He was still angry at Gluskabe. He also wanted to do something great by himself. As they went along they passed another hilltop. A great bird stood on top of that hill, too. As it held its wings open wide, light streamed out.

"Who is that?" Skunk said.

"That is the Day Eagle," said Gluskabe. "While his wings are open it is day. If he closes them it will be night."

Skunk looked and saw it was so. The Day Eagle was beginning to close its wings and evening was beginning. Soon it was so dark they made camp for the night. Gluskabe fell asleep. Skunk, though, did not sleep. He took a ball of rawhide and went to the place where the Day Eagle stood. He bound the great bird's wings so that it could not open them, no matter how hard it tried. Then Skunk sneaked back and pretended to sleep.

When morning came, there was no daylight. The birds and animals were frightened and confused. They wandered around in the darkness. Only Skunk was not afraid. He laughed when he saw how the others acted.

Gluskabe found his way in the dark back to the Day Eagle's hilltop.

"Who has done this to you, Grandfather?" he said.

"It was the white one who travels with you," the Day Eagle said.

Then Gluskabe tried to untie the knots Skunk had tied. They were very tight, so tight Gluskabe could not

6

untie them all. He could only free one of the Day Eagle's wings. To this day the Day Eagle can only open one wing. He keeps it open all the time for fear Skunk will come again. Thus it is that only half the world has daylight at any time for the Day Eagle must keep turning around on his hilltop to share the daylight with all the world.

Gluskabe went back to Skunk. He took his pipe and emptied the ashes over Skunk's head, making his white coat black. With his fingers he drew two white stripes to remind the Skunk of how beautiful he had once been.

"Now everyone will remember what you have done," Gluskabe said. He blew smoke on the Skunk and he became bad-smelling. "Now none of the people will want to be with you."

As the Skunk went away he rubbed off some of his bad scent on the marsh grass. To this day the insects will not eat that kind of grass. But Gluskabe saw what Skunk did. Gluskabe walked into the marsh and breathed on the grass and made it smell pleasant. That is how the sweetgrass came to be and because it was touched by Gluskabe's breath it is one of the sacred plants.

To this day, the Skunk seldom comes out until it is dark. It is not just that he is ashamed of his sooty coat, he also fears the Day Eagle will seek revenge for what he did long ago.

So the story goes.

GLUSKABE MAKES
THE PEOPLE

After Gluskabe had travelled around for some time, he began to notice that something was still missing from the world. He wanted to hear the voices of people.

"It is time," he said, "to make human beings."

So he gathered together some red earth and began to shape it. He formed it just as he had formed himself out of the dust which fell from Tabaldak's hands. First he made a head which was pointing towards the north. To this day the Indian people always sleep with their heads to the north. Then he shaped two arms, one towards the east and one towards the west. Towards the south he made two legs. Last of all, he shaped the body and connected all of the part of the first human together. Finally he breathed upon his creation and the first person became alive and sat up. That person, though, was alone and lonely, even though Gluskabe tried to amuse this new person and keep this first human being company. So Gluskabe had to make another human being. Then, now that there were two people in the world, a woman and a man, they were no longer lonely.

This is one story of how the human beings were made by Gluskabe, but there is another story, too. This story tells how Gluskabe made the first people out of stone. Because they were made of stone they were very strong. They did not need to eat and they never grew tired or slept. Their hearts, too, were made of stone. They began to do cruel things. They killed animals for amusement and pulled trees up by their roots. When Gluskabe saw this he knew he had made a mistake. So he changed them all back into stone. To this day there are certain mountains and hills which look like a sleeping person.

9

Some old people say those are the first ones Gluskabe made, whom he changed back into stone.

Then, instead of making more stone people, Gluskabe looked around for something else to make human beings. He saw the ash trees. They were tall and slender and they danced gracefully in the wind. Then Gluskabe made the shapes of men and women in the trunks of the ash trees. He took out his long bow and arrows and shot the arrows into the ashes. Where each arrow went in a person stepped forth, straight and tall. Those people had hearts which were growing and green. They were the first Abenakis. To this day those who remember this story call the ash trees their relatives.

GLUSKABE CHANGES THE ANIMALS

After Gluskabe made human beings he decided to see how the other creatures would get along with them. He called all of the animals together.

"My friends," he said, "I am going to say a word. When I say that word I want to see what you will do." Then he took a breath and spoke the word which means human beings. "Alnabe," he said.

The rabbits and the deer, the caribou and elk turned and fled into the forest. The wolves and the bears growled and then slipped back into the cover of the trees. Gluskabe nodded. This was how it should be. Almost all of the animals ran and hid when they heard the word for human beings. But not all of the animals ran away. The squirrel and the moose stayed where they were. In those days the squirrel was very large, bigger than the biggest bear. The moose, too, was bigger than it is now. It stood above the biggest trees. Gluskabe raised one eyebrow and looked at the squirrel. "Alnabe," he said again.

When the squirrel heard the word spoken a second time it became very angry. It picked up big rocks and threw them. It tore branches off the trees. Then Gluskabe said the word to the moose. It stomped its huge feet on the earth and knocked trees down with its big horns.

"So," said Gluskabe to the squirrel. "What will you do when you see a human being."

"I will grab any human being I see and tear it apart," the squirrel snarled. "I will kill all the human beings."

Gluskabe shook his head. "No, nijia," he said. "That is not how it will be when you see my children and my children's children." He reached out a hand and picked

11

up the squirrel. With his other hand he began to pet it. As he did so the squirrel grew smaller and smaller until it was littler than the smallest rabbit.

"Now," Gluskabe said, "you will not be able to hurt my people."

Even so, the squirrel still has a bad temper to this day. When you go into his forest he will run around in the treetops throwing twigs down to you and threaten you in his small voice, for he still remembers when he was big and terrible.

Gluskabe turned to the moose. "What will you do when you see a human being?" he said.

The moose shook his antlers. "I will toss him on my horns. I will trample him under my feet."

"No," Gluskabe said, "That is not how it should be." He placed one hand on the moose's head between his horns and the other hand against the moose's nose. "Show me how strong you are, nijia," Gluskabe said. "Push as hard as you can."

The moose pushed. He pushed and pushed and as he pushed he grew smaller. His neck grew shorter and his nose became bent. Then Gluskabe stopped. The moose was still large, but he was no longer a great danger to the people. But to this day the moose has a broken nose and a short neck because of how he pushed and if you look between his horns you can see the mark of Gluskabe's hand.

That is how Gluskabe changed the animals so the world would be better for the people.

13

GLUSKABE AND THE
MAPLE TREES

A long time ago, when the world was new, the Creator made it so that life was very easy for the people. There was plenty of game to hunt and the rivers were filled with fish. The fields by the rivers were fertile for growing corn and beans and squash and the weather was always good. In those days, too, the maple trees were a very special gift from the Creator. They were filled with thick sweet syrup. Whenever anyone wanted to get maple syrup from the trees at any time of the year, all they had to do was break off a twig and collect it as it dripped out.

One day, Gluskabe was walking around. "I think I'll go see how my friends, the human beings are doing," he said. So he went to a village of Indian people. But there was no one around. The lodges looked run down and uncared-for. No one was around making baskets or tanning skins or doing quill work to make beautiful patterns on their clothing. Gluskabe looked hard for the people. They were not fishing in the streams or the lake. They were not hunting for game animals. They were not working in the fields hoeing their crops. In fact, the corn and beans and squash were being crowded out by weeds. They were not gathering berries. They were not wrestling or running races to stay strong. There were not even any children playing.

"This is very strange," Gluskabe said.

Then he thought he heard a noise. It sounded like people sighing in contentment. He followed that noise over the hill and there he found all of the people. They were in the grove of maple trees just over the hill from the village. All of them, the men and women, the boys and girls, the old and the young, were just lying on their

15

backs with their mouths open, letting the maple syrup drip into their mouths. They had grown very fat from all of that sweet maple syrup and they did not even greet Gluskabe. They seemed to be only awake enough to keep their mouths open and swallow.

"This will not do," Gluskabe said. "My people should not be so fat and lazy. I see that when life is too easy they will not care for anyone else."

So Gluskabe took some bark from the birch tree. He fashioned the bark into a bucket which he sewed together with string that he made from the basswood tree and he used pine pitch to make the bucket watertight. He blew on the basket and it grew larger and larger. Then, when it was very big indeed, he went down to the river and dipped in his bucket, filling it with water. He brought that water back to the grove and poured it into the tops of all the maple trees so that it thinned out the syrup. What came out was thin and watery and just barely sweet to the taste. Not only that, it began to flow slower and slower and it became more and more bitter. The people all began to sit up, for the sap was no longer sweet to the taste anymore. They looked at Gluskabe.

"Where has our sweet drink gone?" they said.

"This is how it will be from now on," Gluskabe said. "No longer will syrup drip from the maple trees. Now there will only be this watery sap. When people want to make maple syrup they will have to gather many buckets full of the sap in a birch bark basket like mine. They will have to gather wood and make fires so they can heat stones to drop into the baskets. They will have to boil the water with the heated stones for a long time to make even a little maple syrup. Then my people will no longer grow fat and lazy. Then they will appreciate this maple syrup. Not only that, this sap will only drip from the trees at a certain time of the year. Then it will not keep people from hunting and fishing and gathering

16

and hoeing in the fields and doing all the things that people must do. This is how it is going to be," Gluskabe said.

And so it is to this day.

GLUSKABE AND DZIDZIZ

One day Gluskabe came into his Grandmother's lodge.

"Grandmother," he said, "there is nothing left for me to do. I have conquered all of the monsters. There is no one who can defeat me."

Grandmother Woodchuck shook her head. "That is not so, Grandson. There is one whom you cannot overcome."

"How can this be so?" Gluskabe said. "I have defeated the magician, Grasshopper. I was stronger than Aglebemu, who captured all the water in the world. I tied the wings of the Wind Eagle and transformed the animals. I am sure there is no one on this earth I cannot overcome."

Grandmother Woodchuck shook her head again. "Gluskabe," she said, "soon it will be time for us to leave and let our children and our children's children take care of the earth. This world is changing and there is one whom you cannot defeat. He is called Dzidziz."

"Hunnh," said Gluskabe. "Where can I find this mighty one."

"You can find him near the Place of White Stone. He lives there in the lodge of Nigawes."

So Gluskabe went to the Place of White Stone. There was an Indian village there and he walked into it with his head held high. "Where is Dzidziz?" he said. "I have been told he is in the lodge of Nigawes."

"That is so," said an old woman. "Dzidziz is in that lodge there. You are lucky to have arrived just now. He has just wakened from his nap or you would not be able to see him."

"Is this Dzidziz so mighty that no one dares wake him when he is sleeping?" Gluskabe said.

The old woman smiled. "You might say that."

19

Gluskabe entered the lodge. A woman was sitting by the fire.

"I have come to see Dzidziz," Gluskabe said.

"Kuai!" said the woman. "You are welcome to our lodge. Dzidziz is over there." She motioned with her chin to the other side of the fire. There a small baby was crawling on a blanket made of bearskins. Gluskabe had never seen a baby before and did not know that *dzidziz* is simply the word which means "baby" and that *nigawes* just means mother.

"Kuai!" said Gluskabe to the baby. But Dzidziz did not answer.

"Hunnh," said Gluskabe. "You think you are too strong to answer me. But I command you to do so! Kuai!" But Dzidziz paid no attention. He continued to crawl about on his blanket.

"So," Gluskabe said, "you are challenging me? But I can do anything you can do."

Then Gluskabe crawled around on his hands and knees just as Dzidziz was doing. He did it very well, just as well as the baby. Before long, however, Dzidziz grew tired of crawling. He rolled over onto his back and began to play with his toes.

"Ah-hah," Gluskabe said. "You challenge me again? But I can do this, too."

Then Gluskabe rolled over on his back. He took off his mokasins and began to play with his toes also, watching the baby closely to be sure he did everything just as Dzidziz did. After a while Dzidziz pulled one of his feet up to his mouth and began to suck on his toes.

"You cannot defeat me!" Gluskabe said. He pulled and tugged at his leg and finally got his foot up close enough to his mouth so that he, too, could suck on his toes.

Now, though, Dzidziz grew tired of sucking his toes. He rolled back to his stomach and reached for his favorite toy, a piece of deerskin stuffed and sewed together to look like a turtle.

"Kaamoji!" Gluskabe said. "You are stronger than I thought. Come over here to me!" But Dzidziz paid no attention and started chewing on the leather turtle.

20

Gluskabe bent closer. "Is that when gives you your power?" he said. "Then I will take it from you." He pulled the leather turtle from the baby's hands. As soon as he did so the baby began to cry and scream. Gluskabe had never heard such a sound before. He thought it would break his ears and he covered them with his hands.

"Be silent!" Gluskabe shouted, but Dzidziz did not stop screaming. Then Gluskabe tried singing to the baby. He sang a song powerful enough to calm the strong winds and quiet the most powerful storm. All around the Place of White Stone the winds stopped blowing and the waters became calm. But within the wigwom Dzidziz still screamed.

"You have won," Gluskabe shouted. "Here." He gave the leather turtle back to the baby. But Dzidziz was not yet ready to stop crying. He continued to scream. He clenched his fists and his face grew red. Gluskabe looked around in despair.

"Is no one stronger than Dzidziz," said Gluskabe. "Who can make him stop?"

Then the young woman, who had sat calmly through it all, leaned over and picked up the baby. She placed him on her shoulder and crooned a lullaby. Gradually Dzidziz stopped crying and became quiet. Before long he was asleep.

"Oleohneh," said Gluskabe. "Who are you who can calm the mighty Dzidziz?"

"I am Nigawes," said the woman. "I am his mother and he is my baby. Be quiet or you will wake him up."

Then Gluskabe tiptoed out of the wigwom. He went back to the lodge of his Grandmother Woodchuck.

"Grandmother," Gluskabe said, "you were right. I cannot defeat Dzidziz." Then Gluskabe smiled. "But he, too, is not the mightiest one on earth. Dzidziz is not mightier than Nigawes. The Mother is stronger than the Baby."

And so it is to this day. Nitatci notlokangan wa Gluskabe umetabegesin. And here this story of Gluskabe is ended.

GLUSKABE'S UNCLE TURTLE
AND THE BIRDS

One day that Gluskabe was walking beside the big water. He was feeling hungry and decided to do some fishing. Before long, he caught a giant fish. It was so big that Gluskabe decided to share it and so he went to get his uncle, Tolba the Turtle.

"Come with me, Uncle," Gluskabe said. "There is plenty for us to eat."

When they came back to the big water, Tolba saw that it was so. The fish Gluskabe caught was the biggest one he had ever seen. They made a fire and cooked some of the meat. They both ate as much as they wanted from the great fish and there was still a great deal left.

"You can do as you wish with the rest of this," Gluskabe said. "I am going back to my lodge."

For a time, Turtle sat and looked at the fish. What use could he make of it? Then Turtle had an idea. For a long time he had been wanting a fan made of feathers.

"I think I should share this with my good friends, the birds," Turtle said to himself.

So he did that. He sent out an invitation to all of the birds in the world. When the birds heard they were invited to a great feast, they all came. There were so many in the air that they blocked out the light of the sun. They settled around the great fish and they began to eat. Turtle, however, was not eating. He was looking at all of the birds and deciding which had the finest feathers. There was no doubt—the finest of all were those of the Eagle, Chief of the birds. Turtle sneaked behind the Eagle and cut off his tail feathers. He did it so carefully, that Eagle did not even notice. Then Turtle slipped away, carrying his new feather fan.

The Hawk, who was feeding next to the Eagle looked over at his chief and saw his tail feathers were gone. "Who has done this to you?" the Hawk said. "You are our chief. This is an insult to all of the birds." Eagle looked around. "Where has the Turtle gone?" he said. "He is the one who must have done this. I have heard that he wanted a fan."

Then all the birds looked for Turtle. He was nowhere to be seen. But when they listened, they could hear someone singing a song far away. It was Turtle and he was singing:

His tail is now my fan.
His tail is now my fan.
I have the finest fan of all.
His tail is now my fan.

Then all the birds grew very angry. They decided to find Turtle and kill him and they all flew up in the air to chase him.

Turtle, however, had reached Gluskabe's lodge.

"You must help me, Nephew," Turtle said. "The birds are after me."

Gluskabe saw the fan which Turtle was carrying.

"Uncle," Gluskabe said, "you have done wrong to cut off the Chief's tail. Why should I help you?"

"If you do not help me, they will attack me and kill me," Turtle said.

So Gluskabe agreed to help. He built a nest of sticks high up in a tree.

"Climb up there, Uncle," Gluskabe said. "They will never find you there."

Then Turtle tried to climb up, but he was too awkward.

"Nephew," he said, "My heel claws are too dull. I cannot climb."

So Gluskabe picked Turtle up, tossed him into the nest and then climbed up himself. "Now, Uncle," Gluskabe said, "you must lie still and be very quiet."

Before long, the birds followed Turtle's trail to the

tree. When the trail ended, they did not know where to look and they became discouraged. In the nest high up in the tree, however, Turtle was getting restless.

"Nephew," Turtle said," I cannot stay still."

"Hush," Gluskabe said, "Soon the birds will go away."

But Turtle could not stay still. He moved around in the nest so that the back of his shell was sticking out and he knocked loose a small stick. That stick fell down and landed in front of the Eagle.

"There is our enemy!" the Eagle cried, pointing up into the tree, "that bad one, that coward!" Then Eagle notched an arrow to his bow and fired. The arrow struck the back of Turtle's shell and knocked him right out of the tree. Down Turtle fell, right into some thick brush.

When the birds came to the place where Turtle fell, they could not find him.

"He is gone," they said.

"Look carefully for him," said the Hawk. "He is very clever." Then the Hawk saw an old dirty bark basket on the ground. He walked over to it and kicked it hard, turning it over. As soon as he did that, Turtle stuck out his legs and head and tried to turn over again. "Here he is!" Hawk cried. Then they took Turtle prisoner.

Now the birds were not sure what to do. They wanted to kill Turtle but they couldn't decide on the best way to do it.

"Let us beat him to death," said the Crane.

"That cannot hurt me!" Turtle said, "My back is so strong it will break your clubs."

Then the birds tried to beat him to death, but their clubs broke on Turtle's hard back.

"Let us cut him up into pieces," said the Hawk.

"Hah!" Turtle said. "My shell is too hard for you. No knives can hurt me."

"Let us burn him up in a big fire," said the Eagle.

"Hah!" Turtle said. "Fire cannot kill me. My skin is too tough."

"Perhaps," the Loon said, "we could drown him."

"No," Turtle said. "Do not do that. Water will kill me. Not the water, not the water!"

As soon as Turtle said that, the birds grabbed him. They began to drag him towards the lake. Turtle shouted and struggled. He dug his feet into the earth and tore the ground up so much that the earth near that lake is still furrowed. "Do not drown me," he cried, "do not drown me."

The birds did not listen. They picked him up and threw him into the pond. Back down and belly up, Turtle sank beneath the surface still struggling so much that the waters of the pond became muddy.

"Our enemy is dead," the birds said and they began to rejoice.

Just then, however, Turtle stuck his head out of the water, "Oho!" he shouted to them. "The water is my land. My land doesn't kill me!"

And then he dived beneath the surface and was gone.

But although he escaped, he learned his lesson. To this day, no Turtle has an Eagle feather fan and you will never find a Turtle hiding in a nest in a tree.

GLUSKABE AND THE
FOUR WISHES

Now that Gluskabe had done so many things to make the world a better place for his children and his children's children, he decided it was time for him to rest. He and Grandmother Woodchuck went down to the big water. Gluskabe and his Grandmother climbed into his stone canoe and sailed away to an island. Some say that island is in the great lake the people call Peton-bowk, others say that Gluskabe went far to the east, beyond the coast of Maine. They say that the fog which rises out there is actually the smoke from Gluskabe's pipe. But wherever it is that Gluskabe and Grandmother Woodchuck went to, it is said that for a time Gluskabe let it be known to the world that anyone who came to him would be granted one wish.

Once there were four Abenaki men who decided to make the journey to visit Gluskabe. One of them was a man who had almost no possessions. His wish was that Gluskabe would make it so that he owned many fine things. The second man was a man who was very vain. He was already quite tall, but he wore his hair piled up high on his head and stuffed moss in his mokasins so that he would be even greater in height. His wish was to be taller than all men. A third man was very afraid of dying. His wish was that he would live longer than any man. The fourth man was a man who spent much time hunting to provide food for his family and his village. But he was not a very good hunter, even though he tried very hard. His wish was that he would become a good enough hunter to always give his people enough to eat.

The four of them set out in a canoe to find the island of Gluskabe. Their trip was not an easy one. The currents were strong and they had to paddle hard against

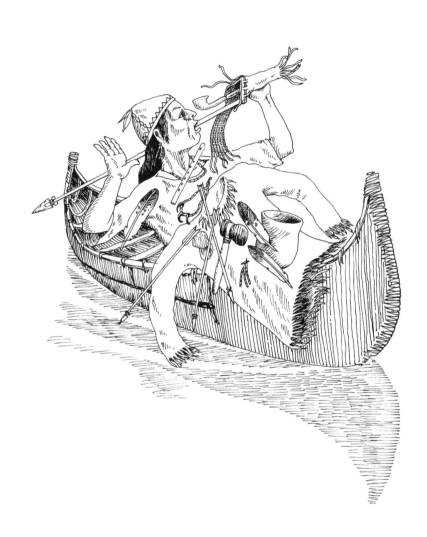

them. The man who owned nothing knew a song to calm the waters and when he sang it the currents ceased and they were able to go on their way. Now a wind began to blow very hard, pushing them back towards shore. But the second man took out some tobacco and offered it to the wind and it became calm enough for them to continue on their way. Soon great whales began to come up near the boat and it seemed as if they would tip the boat over. But the man who was afraid of dying had brought with him a small stone figure shaped like a whale. He dropped it into the water as an offering and the whales dove beneath the surface and were gone. Now the island of Gluskabe was very close, but they could not see it because a fog came up over the ocean and covered everything. The fourth man, who wanted to be a good hunter, took out his pipe and began to smoke it, making an offering of his smoke so that Gluskabe would stop smoking his own pipe and let the fog lift. Soon the fog rolled away and they saw the Island of Gluskabe was there before them.

They left their boat on the shore and made their way to the place where Gluskabe sat.

"Kuai!" Gluskabe said. "You have had to work hard to come here to see me. You have earned the right to each make one wish."

"I wish to own many fine possessions," said the first man.

"My wish is to be taller than any other man," said the second.

"I want to live longer than any man," said the third.

"My desire is not so much for myself," said the fourth man. "I want to be a good enough hunter to provide food for my family and my people."

Gluskabe looked at the fourth man and smiled. Then he took out four pouches and gave one to each of the men. "In these you will find what you want. But do not open them before you get home and in your own lodge."

The men all agreed and went back to their canoe. They crossed the waters and reached the land. Then each of them started on his own way home. The first man, who wanted many possessions, took the canoe which had belonged to the one who wanted to live longer than any man.

"Take this to go home in," said the man who wanted to live long, "I am going to live forever, so it will be easy for me to get another canoe."

As the man who wanted many possessions paddled along he thought about all that he would have. He would have fine clothing of buckskin, he would have ornaments made of shells and bright stones, he would have stone axes and finely made weapons, he would have a beautiful lodge to live in. As he thought of all the things he would have he grew more and more anxious to see them. Finally, he could wait no longer.

"It will not hurt anything if I just peek inside this pouch," he said. Then he opened it just a crack to look inside. As soon as he did so all kinds of things began to pour out of the pouch. Moccasins and shirts, necklaces and wampum belts, axes and spears and bows and arrows. The man tried to close the pouch but he could not do so. The things came pouring out and filled the canoe, covering the man. They were so heavy that the canoe sank and the man, tangled in all his possessions, sank with them and drowned.

The second man, who wanted to be taller than all others, had walked along for only a short time before he, too, became curious. He stopped on top of a high ridge and took out the pouch. "How can this make me taller?" he said. "Perhaps there is some kind of magic ointment in here that I can rub on myself to make me grow. There would be nothing wrong with trying out just a little of it before I get home." Then he opened the pouch. As soon as he did so he was transformed into a pine, the tallest of the trees. To this day the pines stand taller than all others, growing on the high ridges, and in the wind you may hear them whispering, bragging about their height, taller than all men.

The third man, too, did not go far before he became curious. "If I am going to live forever," he said, "then nothing will be able to hurt me. Thus there is no reason why I should not open this pouch." He opened it up. As soon as he did so he turned into a great boulder, one which would stand unchanged for thousands of seasons, longer than the life of any man.

The fourth man, though, did not think of himself as he travelled home. He had further to go than the others, but he did not stop. "Soon," he said to himself, "I will be able to feed my people." He went straight to his lodge and when he got inside he opened the pouch. But there was nothing inside it. Yet as he sat there, holding the open pouch, there came into his mind a great understanding. He realized the ways he must proceed to hunt animals. He began to understand how to prepare himself for a hunt and how to show the animals respect so that they would always allow him to hunt. It seemed he could hear someone speaking to him, more than one person. Then he realized what he was hearing. He was hearing the voices of the animals themselves, telling him about their ways. From that day on he was the best hunter among the people. He never took more game than was needed, yet he always provided enough to feed his people. His was truly the best of the gifts given by Gluskabe.

AZABAN THE RACCOON

I. Raccoon and the Waterfall

Wowigit ndatlokangan wa Azaban. Here camps my story of Azaban.

One day, Azaban the Raccoon was walking around. There were many things which Azaban could have done back at his own lodge. However, those were boring things, everyday things, things which he was supposed to do. Azaban would much rather do things he wasn't supposed to do, especially on a fine day like this one. His long fingers were just itching to get into something. As always, Azaban was looking for trouble.

As he walked along through the woods, he heard the chirping of baby birds from the trees above him.

"Little birds," he called up, "Come down and play with your Uncle Azaban. I will teach you some new games."

The mother birds, though, looked out of their nests with suspicion. They would not let the little birds go and play with Azaban.

"Be careful," they said to their young ones. "Azaban is a nest-robber. You cannot trust him."

"Silly birds," Azaban said to himself. "Don't they know I just like to play with baby birds and birds' eggs. It isn't my fault if playing makes me hungry some times."

He looked up at the trees and smiled, but he could see that he would have no luck there today. The birds were being too watchful.

"Don't worry, little birds," Azaban called back over his shoulder, "I will be back another day."

33

Azaban walked and walked. Soon he was in a valley which led through the hills. Then he cocked his head and listened. He could hear something. It sounded like many people shouting.

"Now what is that?" Azaban said. "I shall have to go and see."

He began to follow the sound, which seemed to be coming from the end of the valley. The closer he came, the louder the sound became. Finally, pushing his way through some brush, Azaban found himself on the edge of a cliff, looking down at the Winooski River where it turned into a great waterfall. Below him the waterfall roared and roared. It made a sound like the voices of many people all shouting together.

"Ah-hunh," said Azaban, speaking to the waterfall. "So you think you can shout loudly, do you?"

The waterfall did not answer him. It just kept pouring down, splashing on the rocks below.

"Do you think you can outshout me?" said Azaban? "I am Azaban, the great one, you know."

But the waterfall still did not answer him.

"Do you think you can ignore me?" Azaban said. "Listen, I shall outshout you!"

Then Azaban shouted. "Yiiiiii!" But his little voice was nowhere near as loud as the waterfall.

"Hmm," Azaban said, "I see that I shall have to shout louder."

He took a deep breath and shouted even more loudly. "YIIIII!" But his little voice was still drowned out by the roar of the waterfall."

"I shall have to get closer," Azaban said. He climbed down closer to the edge of the falls, took a very deep breath and shouted again. "YIIIIIIIIIIII!" But his little voice was still lost in the sound of the falls.

"Hmm," Azaban said, "I shall have to lean out further." Then he took a very very deep breath. He filled his lungs with as much air as he could and shouted. "YIIIIIIIIIIIIIIIIIIII!" He shouted so loud and so long that he became dizzy and lost his balance. Down he fell, into the water. Before he could rescue himself he was swept over the falls.

II. Raccoon and the Two Sisters

Further down that same river, two old sisters lived in a little lodge close to the water. They had placed their lodge there because they wanted to be close to their fish traps which they had placed in the water. These two sisters were very strange. They had only one eye between the two of them. Whenever one of them wanted to see, she would hold out her hand and say, "Sister, give me the eye." Then the old woman who had the eye would pluck it out of her head and give it to her sister. So it was that one of them was always blind and one of them could always see.

In order to make their lives easier and to help whichever of the sisters was blind while the other one had the eye, they had made ropes out of twisted milkweed fibers and strung them all around to guide them in their daily chores. One rope led from the lodge down to the river and the fishtraps. Another rope led to their cooking pot and the rough hearth in front of their lodge. Yet another rope led to the spring where they got clean water to drink, not wanting to use the muddy water from the river. It just so happened that day that the one sister who had the eye was down checking the fish traps when she saw something floating down stream.

"Sister," she called, "I see something floating our way."

"Is it something good to eat?" called back the blind sister who was sitting up by the lodge.

"It looks like a dead raccoon," said the sister with the eye. Then she reached out and grabbed Azaban as he floated by. "It is a dead raccoon," she said. "It is a very ugly and skinny one. It looks like it has been dead a long time. But I think it will still give us a meal."

The sister with the eye carried Azaban back to their cooking pot. There she took off his skin, and dropped him in the water. Before long the water was boiling and the smell of raccoon soup was filling the air. Just then,

35

Azaban, began to wake up. He was not dead at all, he had only been knocked unconscious when he went over the waterfall.

"What is that I smell?" he said. "That smells like soup. Mmmm, I love soup. I wonder what kind is it? Is it venison? No, that's not it? Bear? Noooo. Beaver tail? Noooo, not that. Ah, I know what it is. It is Raccoon soup. Raccoon?"

Azaban looked around. He saw where he was, inside a cooking pot. Not only that, his skin was gone. And there it was, hanging from a pole, Just then, the one old sister who had the eye leaned over to look into the pot to see how their meal was cooking. Azaban splashed the hot water at her and she jumped back with a shout.

"What is wrong, sister?" said the blind one.

"Our food has splashed water on me," said the one with the eye.

"That cannot be," said the blind one. "Sister, give me the eye! I want to take a look."

Then the sister with their one eye took the eye out and handed it over towards her blind sister. The blind sister put the eye in and leaned over the pot. Azaban splashed water at her, too, and she jumped back.

"What is wrong, sister?"

"Our food has splashed me, too!"

While they were talking, Azaban, crawled out of the pot. He sneaked behind the sister with the eye — for he had seen what they were doing — and tapped her on the back.

"Sister," Azaban said, imitating the voice of an old woman, "give me the eye. I want to look at our food."

He reached out his paw — which was just like the skinny hand of an old woman. Without looking, the old sister pulled out the eye and placed it in Azaban's paw.

"Now can you see our food?" said the first old sister.

"I can't see it until you give me our eye," said the second one.

"I have already given it to you," said the first one.

"No, you have not," said the second.

While they were arguing, Azaban went over to the pole where his skin was hanging. He climbed up, unhooked it, and slipped it back on. Then he sat down and watched. Things were getting interesting.

"You are trying to keep our eye for yourself," said the first sister.

"You are the one who is trying to keep it," said the second one.

"I am not going to argue with you anymore," said the first one.

It looked as if they were going to end their argument. That didn't please Azaban. He stepped in between the two sisters and slapped the first one.

"Ah," she said. "Why did you hit me, sister?"

Then Azaban reached up and slapped the second sister.

"Ah, why did *you* hit me?" the second one said. The two old sisters then began to fight with each other. Finally they knocked over the pot, spilling out all the water.

"Now you have done it," said the first sister, feeling around with her hands. "First you lost our eye. Now you've spilled our pot and I cannot find our food."

"Let's stop arguing. I am too hungry. You go to the spring and get more water," said the second sister. "I will go down to the river and check our fish traps for something we can eat."

Then each of the sisters began to follow the ropes which would lead them to the places they wished to go. But Azaban was ahead of them. He had untied the cord which led to a sapling by the spring and retied it to a little tree next to a pile of sand. He had untied the cord which led down to the river and retied it so that it ended in a patch of briers. He leaned against the wall of the lodge and waited. Before long the first sister came back, her water pot filled with sand that she had dipped from the sandpile. Then the second sister came back with her hands all scratched.

"The river has gone dry," said the second sister. "It has all grown up with briers."

38

"What do you mean?" said the first sister. "You just didn't want to walk all that way to check the fish traps. You are getting lazy. But I brought back this water to cook with."

The second sister took the water pot and felt inside. "This is filled with sand," she said. "Why are you trying to play tricks on me."

"You are the one who is playing tricks," said the first sister.

"No, I am not," said the second one.

So they argued until Azaban finally grew tired of listening to them. He placed their one eye down where he knew they would eventually find it on a log near the entrance to their lodge. Then he went off in search of something else interesting to do.

III. Raccoon and the Crayfish

As Azaban walked along down the river he began to feel hungry. Then he noticed a crayfish scooting under a rock in the stream next to him.

"Hmm," Azaban said, "I think I will see what my friend there is doing under that stone."

He waded into the stream and began to feel around with his long fingers. But the crayfish, when it saw Azaban's fingers grasping for him reached out one claw and pinched Azaban very hard on one of his fingers. Azaban snatched his hand back.

"Ahhh!" he said. "My friend does not want to come out and see me." Then Azaban thought about what he could do. He was very hungry now but he didn't want to get pinched again. He walked out of the stream and stood on the stream bank.

"Ohhh," he moaned, "Look at me. I am nothing but skin and bones. I am weak and sick from hunger. I am so hungry that I am about to starve. In fact, I am going to die right now." Then Azaban fell down on the ground, rolled over on his back and stuck his feet up in the air.

After a while, the crayfish which had been hiding under the rock stuck its head out of the stream to see what was going on. There lay Azaban, right next to the stream. The crayfish ducked back into the water, but no long raccoon fingers came reaching in after him. Again he stuck his head out to look. The raccoon had not moved! The crayfish crawled out to look. Azaban lay there with his feet straight up and his mouth open. Perhaps he really had died. The crayfish crawled closer. It was just as the raccoon had said. He was very skinny and sick-looking. He was really dead! The crayfish scuttled back into the stream and went to tell the other crayfish that their great enemy had died.

41

"How has this happened that the Man-Eater is dead?" said the old sachem of the crayfish.

"Ah," said the little crayfish, "the Man-Eater tried to eat me. But I fought with him. Yes! I fought long and hard. Finally I threw him down to the ground and he was dead."

"Hmmm," said the old sachem of the crayfish. "We must go and see if this is so."

Before long, all the crayfish had gathered in the stream near Azaban's body. They were ready to climb out of the water to jeer at their great enemy. But one wise old sachem crayfish would not let them go too close.

"We must make sure the Man-Eater is truly dead," said the old sachem crayfish. "You! Go and pinch his tail."

So one of the young warrior crayfish scuttled over, pinched Azaban's tail and scooted back quickly. Azaban's feet twitched just a little when his tail was pinched, but none of the crayfish noticed.

"He *is* dead," said the young warrior crayfish.

"Go and pinch his nose," said the old sachem crayfish.

Then the young warrior crayfish scuttled up and pinched Azaban's nose very hard, twisting his claw as he did it. Azaban's mouth opened a little wider when his nose was pinched, but none of the crayfish noticed.

"There is no doubt," the young warrior crayfish said, "our great enemy has died."

Then all the crayfish came out of the stream. They made a great circle around Azaban's body and began a victory dance. They danced and danced, getting closer to Azaban as they did so. They danced until their little legs were very tired and they could hardly move. Then, Azaban leaped to his feet. He grabbed to the left and to the right, in front of him and behind him. He caught every one of the crayfish and ate them. Then he lay down and went to sleep. When he woke up he smiled.

"My friends, the crayfish," he said. "Thank you for your hospitality. But now I have to go further along my way. I am sure there are other people who want to make me welcome."

Then he turned away from the stream and began to walk.

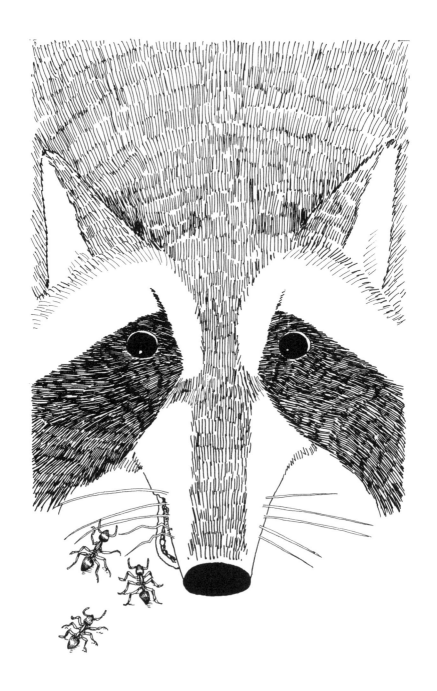

Before too long, Azaban came to the foot of a big hill. He thought he could see someone on that hilltop.

"I wonder who that is up there," Azaban said. "They probably are in need of company." So Azaban began to climb. It took him quite a while to reach the top and by the time he got up there he was feeling very proud of himself for climbing so high. He wanted to boast, but he saw no one else around. Then he noticed the big rock balanced on top of that hill. That rock was what he had seen on the hilltop.

"Grandfather," Azaban said to the Big Rock, "do you see how I have climbed all the way up this mountain. Is it not wonderful?"

"I see, Grandson," said the Big Rock. "It is wonderful indeed how you have climbed up here."

Now Raccoon felt even more boastful. "Yes, and not only am I good at climbing up, I can go down even faster."

"I am sure you can, Grandson," said the Big Rock.

"Grandfather," said Azaban, "don't you get tired of always sitting up here? How would you like to go down the mountain and see a new place?"

"Grandson," said the Big Rock, "I have been sitting here for a long long time. I am not sure that I want to travel. And even if I did, I cannot move by myself. And once I start rolling, it will be hard for me to stop."

"Don't worry, Grandfather, said Azaban. "I will help you." He was eager to prove that he would be able to run down hill even faster than the Big Rock could roll. "Then we can race."

Azaban went and found a long dead tree limb. He wedged it under the Big Rock and pushed. The Big Rock began to rock back and forth.

"Grandson," said the Big Rock, "I am not sure that I want to travel."

But Azaban paid no attention. He pushed and pushed and when the Big Rock had leaned over far enough it began to roll. Down the hill it went, making a great noise. "BADAROOM, BADAROOM, BADAROOM."

"Ah," Azaban shouted, "This is fine!" Then he ran as fast as he could and caught up with the Big Rock. He was, indeed, just as fast. He ran next to the Big Rock, keeping up.

"You see, Grandfather," Azaban shouted, "I am as fast as you are."

But the Big Rock said nothing. It just kept rolling, "BADAROOM, BADAROOM, BADAROOM, BADA-ROOM."

Now Azaban ran in front of the Big Rock. "You see, Grandfather," he shouted, "I am faster than you!"

The Big Rock, though, said nothing. It just kept rolling, "BADAROOM, BADAROOM, BADAROOM, BADAROOM, BADAROOM."

Then Azaban decided to show off. He began to zigzag back and forth in front of the Big Rock.

"You are very slow, Grandfather," Azaban laughed as he darted back and forth.

Just then, though, Azaban caught his foot on a root and fell. Tabat!

But the Big Rock could not stop. It rolled right over Azaban. WHUMP! Then the Big Rock rolled on, leaving the raccoon flattened out.

Azaban was so flat that he couldn't even breathe. He couldn't manage to do more than whisper in a small, small voice for help.

"kgamo, kgamo, kgamo, kgamo . . ." he whispered.

His voice was so small that it was a long time before anyone could hear him and then it was the tiny ants who came.

"You ants," Azaban whispered, "come and help me."

"How can we help the Great Azaban," the ants said, "we are too small. All of the animals say that we are useless little people."

"Ah," Azaban said, "you are small, but there are many of you. If you work together you can do great things. That is why I always have said that the ants are the greatest of all the people. I am sure you can help me."

So the ants began to work. They pushed and pulled and pried. They put Azaban back together as best they could. When they were done, though, he was much flatter to the ground than he had been and he no longer could run as fast. To this day, though, when Raccoon hears a loud noise — like the rumbling of a big rolling stone, he will run up a tree just as quickly as he can.

As soon as those ants had put Azaban back together he looked down at them and said, "Go away, you ants. I have no time for useless little people like you." Then he went walking along his way, leaving the ants feeling very angry at him.

Now there were more things that happened to Azaban, but as my grandfather said to me, that is another tale. Ndatlokangan tagagabesit nimsiwi. That is as far as my story goes.

PMOLA AND THE HUNTER

Once, long ago, a man went hunting. He had been out a long time and had seen nothing. At last he came to the banks of the river. He was tired and thirsty, so he sat down by the water and bent over to take a drink where the water was very still and he could see his face reflected back. But as he bent close, he could see something else reflected in the water. It was the shape that looked like a human being and also did not look like a human being. It had wings and it was high up in the sky and coming closer. The man knew immediately who it was. It was Pmola, a very powerful being.

"Ah," the man said to himself, "I am not certain that I want my friend, Pmola, to see me." He looked around and saw a space where he could hide himself beneath a shelving rock near the stream. He could still see the stream clearly, however.

Soon, with a great flutter of wings, Pmola landed right where the hunter had been. He looked around, but could see nothing. Then, as the hunter watched, Pmola bent over close to the stream.

"Ah," the hunter said to himself, "So my friend drinks water just as I do."

But Pmola did not drink right away. Instead, he placed his hand into his mouth and pulled out a ring. The ring shone like the sunlight and Pmola placed it carefully on a stone behind him. Then he leaned down to the water and began to drink.

When the man saw the shining ring, he knew what he wanted to do. Pmola was said to be *Ktchi medawlinno*, one with great powers and the man was certain that the ring was part of the creature's magic. He crawled flat on his belly, until he reached the stone. Pmola continued drinking, not noticing the hunter who grabbed the ring and quickly crawled back to his hiding place.

As soon as Pmola finished drinking he turned and reached for his ring. It was not there.

"What has happened?" Pmola said in a loud voice. But the hunter said nothing and the creature did not hear him. "So," Pmola said, "it has been stolen from me." Then Pmola began to walk around, but he could not find his ring. In his hiding place, the hunter kept very quiet. "Hear me, my friend," Pmola said, "give me back that which you took. You cannot make any good use of it, but it is my life. Without it I cannot stop very long anywhere. Return it to me and you will have good luck, you will never lack good hunting."

Hearing that, the hunter answered from his hiding place. "I will give this back to you," he said. "But I ask that you do not cheat me."

"My friend," Pmola answered, his voice like the rumble of thunder, "I cannot cheat you if you are not afraid of me."

Then the hunter stood up from his hiding place. He handed the ring back to Pmola.

"Mount upon my back," Pmola said, bending down, "Hold tight, for we will go fast!"

The man climbed on and Pmola spread his mighty wings and rose up into the air. They flew faster than the wind and soon they were in Pmolaki, the creature's own land. It was in that land that the greatest medawlinnos gathered together just when the sun was at its height. All of them were sleeping as Pmola landed and the hunter climbed down from his back.

"Now, my friend," Pmola said, "you must hunt here. There are beavers and otters here. After you have hunted, skin your game and bundle up their hides well. I shall meet you here after the sun has made one move across the sky. But you must be ready then, for the ones who are sleeping will wake up then."

The man did as Pmola told him. He hunted for the otters and the beaver. He watched the sky closely as he skinned them out and bundled them together and he was back at the spot before the sun had moved the width of one hand across the sky. He looked around, but there was no sign of his friend. Now the earth began to tremble beneath his feet and he knew the medawlinnos were beginning to wake up.

"It is true," he said, "what my friend told me."

Now a great noise began to be heard and the ground shook harder. It shook so hard that the hunter was certain the world was about to end. But just as he was about to give up hope, he saw Pmola coming, leaping across the sky.

"Quickly," Pmola said, landing in front of the hunter, "jump upon my back. It is time. The medawlinnos wake up."

Then the hunter leaped upon Pmola's back, holding tightly to the bundles of skins. Up and across the sky they flew, so fast that the hunter could only just imagine it. Soon they landed once again in the hunter's own country.

"Now," Pmola said, "we shall never see each other again, my friend. But you will always have good fortune. You will live long."

And so it happened and so this story ends.

THE FAITHFUL HUNTER

In the old days it was the custom for a man to take his family during the winter months deep into the woods where he would hunt for meat. It happened that a man did so, going far to the north with his family to a place on an island where they began to make their wigwom. A storm began to come up, so the man hurried to get his canoe up from the beach. Just as he was bringing it up through some spruce trees, the wind blew very hard and the man stumbled against a sharp branch which struck him in the chest. He fell down and the canoe fell over him. As soon as he had fallen, though, he found that the pain went away and he could stand up again. He came out from under the canoe and went back to help his wife and children finish building the wigwom. His wife spoke to him, but he said nothing. His children asked him to tell them a story, but he did not speak. Instead he lay down in the other side of the fire from them throughout the night.

So it went all that winter. He spoke to no one, but slept each night alone on the other side of the fire. He hunted each day and his luck was good. He brought his wife and children all that they needed.

At last the spring came and the ice was gone from the river. For the first time the man spoke to his wife. "Take this new canoe I have built," he said. "Go downstream for three days and you will meet your relatives. I must stay here. But after you have found your relatives come back here and you will find me."

The wife did as he said and went downstream. At the end of three days she found her relatives and they returned to the island. They went to the place her husband had told her to go and found the old canoe. When they turned it over, there was the body of her husband, the faithful hunter. He had been dead for a long time. A sharp spruce branch had pierced his heart.

THE DEER WIFE

There once was a man called Zazigoda or The Lazy One. Whenever he went hunting with the other men he would find a place and go to sleep while the other men looked for game. One day, while they were hunting deep in the woods the other men said, "Where is Zazigoda?" They went and looked and found him asleep under a cedar tree. They were tired now of his being so lazy. They went away and left him there.

When Zazigoda awoke it was very dark. He was hungry, but he had no food. He was not sure how to find his way out of the woods because he had always been careless about tracking, only following the other hunters. "Here is where I shall starve," he said. "This is because I have not helped others."

Then, suddenly, there was a woman there. She was dressed in brown deerskin and her hair was long and brown. "Come with me," she said and Zazigoda followed her to her lodge deep in the woods. She gave him food and took care of him. The next day she told him how to hunt for moose. "Wait by the lake. Sing this song," she said, "Then blow through this birchbark horn. The moose will come to you and you can shoot it with your arrows." He went out and did as she told him and that night they feasted on the meat of the moose and she made him a robe of the moose skin. The following day she told him how to hunt for bear. "Go to the berry bushes. Sing this song and wait by the trail. The bear will come to you and you can shoot it with your arrows." Again Zazigoda did as she said. That night they ate bear meat and his wife made for him a robe from the bear skin.

So it went for a long time. Zazigoda grew fat and the lodge was filled with skins. His wife told him how to hunt for every animal in the forest except one. "You

must not hunt for the deer, my husband," she told him and Zazigoda agreed.

At last Zazigoda became lonely for his people. "I must go and visit them," he said. "Go ahead," said his wife, "But I shall remain here. Take the skins and the meat with you and share it with the people. Say nothing about me. Stay until it is the time again for hunting and then come back to me."

Zazigoda did as she said. His relatives rejoiced when they saw him coming with the meat and all the skins. He was a different looking man now. The unmarried women all wanted to dance with him, but Zazigoda paid no attention to them. He stayed, sharing all that he had with the people and then, when the season to hunt came again, he went alone into the woods to the lodge of his wife. He hunted throughout the winter and when spring came his wife gave birth to a daughter. Once more his wife told him to take the food and furs to his relatives and once again she stayed in the woods, this time with their child. Again his relatives were happy to see him and again many of the unmarried women wanted to marry him. All of his relatives told him that a fine man such as he should marry. He refused them three times, but finally on the fourth time he consented. He married one of the women in the village and for a time they lived together happily. But when the season to hunt came he went again into the woods.

When he came to the lodge of his forest wife, he found it was empty. He called and there was no answer. Then he saw her standing at the edge of the forest.

"You have forgotten me," she said. "No longer can I live with you. You will still be able to hunt as you did before, but never must you kill a deer." Then she was gone.

The man was sad to see his wife go and not to see their baby daughter, but he did as she said. He hunted and stayed alone in the lodge and killed many animals, but never killed a deer. He went back with the meat and skins to his wife in the village. She was not pleased.

"Why have you brought me no deer meat?" she said. "That is all that I want."

He tried to refuse, but she continued to ask and beg him. Even his relatives told him that he should do as his wife asked. At last he went and did as she said. He went into the woods to hunt deer. He saw a doe and a fawn and shot the fawn with his arrow. Suddenly his forest wife was there standing before him.

"You have done as I asked you never to do," she said. "Now you have killed our daughter."

Zazigoda looked down and saw that it was so. He turned to his wife but she was running away from him. When he tried to follow her she turned into a deer and disappeared into the cedars.

HOW INDIAN SUMMER
CAME TO BE

Long ago there was a man who was known as Notkikad. This man was a good husband and father and worked hard for his family. He planted a great deal every year and cared for his gardens so that there would be plenty of food. He was always grateful to Tabaldak, The Master of Life, and gave thanks each harvest. One year, though, things did not go well for him. There was a late frost and his garden was killed. He planted it again and then there came a drought. Again he planted, but now it was the autumn and the cold weather came and killed the plants before they were ripe.

Notkikad was very troubled. His wife and children had gathered berries and other foods from the forest, but without the dried corn and squash and beans for them to keep over the long cold time, he was afraid they would not survive. Now the cold season was here and the leaves were falling from the trees and the freezing winds blew. What could he do?

That night, before he slept, he made a small fire and offered tobacco to The Master of Life. "I have never asked for help," he said, "I have always been thankful for the blessings given to me. But now I am troubled, not so much for myself as for my wife and children. I want to know what I can do." Then he went to bed and dreamed.

In his dream The Master came to him. "I am giving you these special seeds," The Master said. "I am also giving you a time in which to plant them."

When Notkikad awoke he found the seeds were there beside him. He went outside and though the leaves were still falling from the trees, the weather was now warm and pleasant as if it were the summer. With the help of

his wife and children he prepared the soil and planted all the seeds. The sun set and rose and the seeds had already germinated and lifted green shoots out of the earth. The sun rose and set again and now the young plants were already waist-high. So it went from day to day as the special seeds given to him grew rapidly in that special time, producing a full crop in the space of only a handful of days. Then Notkikad harvested his crop and dried the corn and beans and squash for the winter. He and his family stored all of the food within their wigwom. Then, as suddenly as it had gone away, the cold winds returned and that special season given by The Master of Life was gone.

To this day, the people say, that special time is still given to us each year, even though we have none of those magical seeds. That time, which people call Indian Summer today, was called Nibunalnoba or "a man's summer" by the Abenaki. It reminds them to always be thankful.